WITHDRAWN
3 4028 02761 8132

SEP 1 6 1997
FB
There's A Branch
Near You
HARRIS COUNTY PUBLIC LIBRARY
HOUSTON, TEXAS

Mr. Pak Buys a Story

Carol Farley

illustrated by Benrei Huang

Albert Whitman & Company

Morton Grove, Illinois

To Sue Alexander,
because her stories are *always* very good.
-C. F.

To Aunt Su-yu, for being great company.
-B. H.

Library of Congress Cataloging-in-Publication Data

Farley, Carol J.
Mr. Pak buys a story/written by Carol Farley;
illustrated by Benrei Huang.
p. cm.

Summary: The unusual story that a wealthy couple's servant
buys from a thief proves to be well worth the price.

ISBN 0-8075-5178-3
[1. Folklore-Korea.] I. Huang, Benrei, ill. II. Title.
PZ8.1.F222Mr 1997
398.2'0951902-dc20 96-34411
CIP AC

 Published
in 1997 by Albert Whitman & Company, 6340 Oakton Street,
Morton Grove, Illinois 60053-2723. Published simultaneously
in Canada by General Publishing, Limited, Toronto.

Printed in the United States of America.
10 9 8 7 6 5 4 3 2 1

Design by Scott Piehl
Text set in Lucidia Casual
Art media: acrylic paint & colored pencil

In 1978, when I taught at Hanyang University in Seoul, Korea, my students would often share their favorite folktales. One that I particularly enjoyed concerned an old farm couple who bought a strange story.

I knew about story selling since it is discussed by William Elliot Griffis in one of the first Korean histories written by an American. In *Corea, the Hermit Nation* (New York: AMS Press, 1971), Griffis writes about poets and "reciters" who wandered from village to village in ancient times, entertaining audiences. People who listened would pay a small sum, and the best reciters would be invited to perform privately. From other sources, I learned that storytellers often used the words "when tigers smoked long pipes" to signify that their tales were make-believe.

I had hoped to find the story in written form, but many Korean tales have never been translated into English. Finally, however, I located a version in a book by Frances Carpenter, *Tales of a Korean Grandmother* (Tokyo: Charles E. Tuttle Company, Inc., 1973). This book contains stories the author collected from travelers who visited or lived in Korea in the late nineteenth century, when the "hermit nation" first opened its borders to the western world.

-Carol Farley

When tigers smoked long pipes, an old man and his wife lived in the land of Korea. They were far from any village or city, and their only company was their faithful servant, Mr. Pak. They were healthy and wealthy, but they were often bored on long evenings.

"If only we knew a good story!" Mr. Kim would say. "Then we could have entertainment."

Mr. Pak was sorry that the couple had nothing to amuse them. "No storyteller will ever come this far out into the countryside," he said. "Perhaps I should go to the city and buy a story."

"What a fine idea!" said Mr. Kim. He placed one hundred gold coins in a money box and gave it to Mr. Pak. "Please buy us a *very* good story and learn it by heart."

So Mr. Pak set out. After several days, he came to the outskirts of the city and approached a man who was walking alone.

"Do you have a story for sale?" Mr. Pak asked, jingling the coins in his money box.

The man was a cunning thief who instantly saw that Mr. Pak had more money than sense. "Yes," he said. "I have a fine story I might sell. How much will you pay?"

"One hundred gold coins," answered Mr. Pak.

The thief's heart leaped. "One hundred gold coins?" he cried. "I'll take it."

"Is *your* story a *very* good one?" asked Mr. Pak.

Nearly choking with greed, the thief replied, "Oh, have no fear. My story is good, all right. Give me the money."

"No," said Mr. Pak. "First I must hear the story."

The thief knew he had to tell some sort of tale. But he could not think of any. He looked around in desperation and spied a stork that had just landed in a rice field. He decided simply to describe what the bird was doing.

"He steps carefully," the thief said. "He comes closer."

This beginning seemed odd to Mr. Pak, but he dutifully repeated the words. "He steps carefully. He comes closer."

"Now he stops and raises his head," the thief said.

"Now he stops and raises his head," said Mr. Pak.

The thief saw the bird pecking at the ground. "He bends down! Now he creeps forward."

This seemed a *most* peculiar story! But Mr. Pak nodded and echoed, "He bends down. Now he creeps forward."

Suddenly a fox appeared behind the bird.
"There's danger!" shouted the thief.
Mr. Pak yelled, too. "Danger!"

But the stork had seen the danger. Flapping its mighty wings, it flew off to safety. “He’s fleeing! All is safe!” the thief cried.

"He's fleeing! All is safe!" Mr. Pak eagerly waited for more. When nothing came, he leaned closer. "Is that the end?"

"Of course!" said the thief. "And a *very* good story it is. Now give me the money."

Mr. Pak handed over the money. He was truly puzzled by the strange story, but surely Mr. Kim would know what it meant.

When Mr. Pak returned to Mr. Kim and his wife, they were happy to finally have some entertainment. But they, too, thought the story was strange. Every night Mr. Kim loudly retold it. His wife and Mr. Pak listened and thought very hard and wondered what the tale could mean. "Tell it again," they would plead.

Many moons later, the thief joined a band of robbers, and they went roving deep into the countryside. The thief had forgotten all about Mr. Pak and the foolish story he had sold him.

One night the robbers came to the house of old Mr. Kim. The thief was eager to show his skill. He quickly started climbing the wall. "I can rob this house alone," he called to the others.

The thief dropped down into Mr. Kim's courtyard. He tiptoed toward the house.

"He steps carefully!" a voice rang out. "He comes closer!"

The thief stopped short. He peered around the courtyard. Had someone seen him?

"Now he stops and raises his head!" cried the voice.

What magic was this? The thief could see no one, but someone could certainly see *him*.

He hunched over, trying to hide himself.

"He bends down!" the voice shouted.

The thief's heart thumped as loudly as the drum of a monk. Perhaps if he crouched closer to the ground, he would not be noticed. He moved slowly toward the house.

"Now he creeps forward!" the voice shouted.

Horrified, the thief leaped up.

"Danger!" cried the voice.

The robber waited no longer. He whirled around and scrambled toward the wall.

"He's fleeing! All is safe!" the voice shouted after him.

The thief nearly flew to the top of the wall. "Run!" he screamed down to his friends. "There's terrible magic here!"

And run they did!

The robbers never returned. Every evening Mr. Kim and his wife continued to sit with Mr. Pak and marvel over the strange story.

"Do you think we paid too much for it?" Mr. Kim would ask from time to time.

"No," his wife would answer. "The more I hear the tale, the more I wonder. And wonder is a very valuable thing."

So they lived happily ever after, never knowing just how *very* good their story was.